STALKED BY THE UMPIRE

EMMA BRAY

CHAPTER
ONE

Jake

I CALL 'em like I see 'em—that's my creed. No gray areas, just the clear-cut line between strike and ball, and it's my sharp eye that draws it. But as I stand there on the edge of the field, whistle around my neck, cap shading my eyes from the glare of the afternoon sun, I can't shake this gnawing feeling in my gut. It's not the usual pre-game jitters or the lingering after-taste of last night's beer. It's emptiness, a hollow pang that not even the roar of the crowd can fill.

"Strike!" My voice cuts through the stadium's

din, decisive, a reflex honed over years in umpire's gear. The batter scowls, but the call stands. Life's full of strikes and balls, and lately, it feels like I'm caught in a count I can't win. The game moves on, players slide and swing, and cheers erupt. They're here for the thrill, the love of the game.

Me? I'm just the guy making the tough calls, invisible until they disagree.

"Out!" I signal with a confidence I don't feel inside. Funny how you can be at the top of your game, respected, even envied, and still come up empty when the lights go out and the stands empty. It's like every time I walk off the field, I leave a piece of me behind, buried in the diamond dust.

"Good call, Reynolds!" someone shouts from the dugout, but the praise feels distant, like applause for someone else. What am I doing here? Where's the rush, the passion I used to have? I've got friends, sure. Nate Hawkins, the golden boy with his mansion and his carefree laugh—he thinks I've got it made. If only he knew how much I crave something...more. Something real that makes my heart pound harder than any close play at the plate.

"Time!" I call out, signaling a brief pause in

the game. I use the moment to steal a breath, to remind myself why I do this. For a split second, the field blurs into a canvas of green and brown, players mere smudges under the bright lights. The scent of fresh grass, the taste of dust—it's all part of me, yet I'm apart from it, an observer in my own life.

It's time to face it: I'm Jake Reynolds, master of the diamond, yet a rookie when it comes to figuring out my own damn desires. I can spot a foul a mile away, but happiness? That's one call I can't seem to make.

———

The sun scorches, but the water in Nate's pool glimmers like some kind of oasis. I'm leaning against the bar, nursing a cold beer when she bursts into the scene—Kaitlyn, Nate's kid sister, now not so much a kid. She's all grown up, and damn, does she make an impression.

"Hey Jake!" she beams, that same bright smile I remember from when she was knee-high to a grasshopper, but everything else...everything else is different.

"Kaitlyn," I say, pushing my voice to sound

casual, cool. But inside? Inside's a whole different ballgame.

She's laughing, tossing her head back, and her blonde hair catches the light like spun silk. Her skin's got this glow, like she's lit from within, and it's hard not to stare at the way the water clings to her curves as she steps out of the pool. She's a vision, no two ways about it, and my body's reaction is primitive, immediate.

"Long time, no see," she says, and there's an edge of something like flirtation in her voice that sends a shockwave straight through me.

"Too long," I manage to get out, even though every alarm bell in my head is ringing *'no way, no way, no way.' She's Nate's sister. She's eighteen. That's a line you don't cross, especially not with your best friend's family.*

"Enjoying the party?" she asks, her hazel eyes sparkling with mischief.

"Sure," I reply, but I'm not really seeing the party, not anymore. It's like she's the only one here, the rest just background noise.

"Come on," she urges, grabbing my hand with a wet, cool touch. "Let's go for a swim."

"Can't," I say quickly, too quickly maybe. "Gotta keep an eye on the game." What game?

There's some sort of volleyball thing happening in the pool, but hell if I can focus on that now.

"Your loss," she teases with a pout that should be illegal, and then she dives back into the blue, leaving me standing there feeling like someone's cranked the heat up another ten degrees.

I take another long gulp of my beer. But it doesn't help. Not one bit. Because Kaitlyn Hawkins has done the impossible—she's made me, the professional umpire and master of self-control, completely and utterly lose my cool.

My cock is so hard I'm sure I could split wood with it. My breathing hitches as I watch her swimming in the pool. She's not wearing a skimpy bikini like the rest of the girls here. No, she's got on this little one-piece that I swear is somehow more alluring than all the other bathing suits in the pool.

My face starts getting red as I worry my erection is noticeable. I try to think of anything else to make it go down.

Peanut butter and jelly. Baby kittens.

Jesus Christ, the way the water trickles down Kaitlyn's belly button…

Fucking hell.

I head to the bathroom.

Once inside the dimly lit bathroom, I lock the door behind me and lean against it, trying to catch my breath. The cool marble under my hands does little to soothe the heat raging through my veins. My heart is hammering, pounding loud in my ears as images of Kaitlyn in that enticing swimsuit play on a loop in my mind.

I close my eyes, inhaling deeply, feeling every inch of tension in my body. The way she moved in the water, like a siren luring me into depths unknown—God, I'm struggling here. Each ripple in the water accentuated her curves, her skin glistening with droplets that traced paths I was desperate to follow with my tongue.

I unzip my jeans, the fabric tight around me, constraining like a vice. My hand slips inside, finding heated flesh that throbs under my touch. The thought of her lips parted in a silent moan as the water enveloped her sends a shiver down my spine. I can almost taste the chlorine on her skin, mixed with the sweet hint of her sweat from lying in the sun. It's intoxicating.

Imagining her stepping out of the pool, water cascading off her like some goddess of the sea, makes my hand move faster. Her hair would be slicked back, drops catching on those long lashes as she blinks up at me. And that smile—that damn mischievous smile—as if she knows exactly where my dirty thoughts are going.

I think about her coming closer, those small droplets now jewels adorning her skin. She'd stand there, inches away, heat radiating between us despite the coolness of the tiles under our feet. Maybe she'd bite her lip slightly, teasingly, knowing all too well how much I want to taste it, to taste *her*.

The fantasy spirals deeper as I envision sliding my fingers along those wet trails on her body, tracing each curve and dip like a map to paradise. The sounds escaping from me blend with imagined soft moans from her lips—her voice a sweet melody that pushes me closer to the edge.

My breathing becomes ragged as pleasure mounts, building up like a crescendo until there's no holding back. I grunt as I come harder than I think I've ever come, white fluid spraying onto the floor. With each pulse and throb beneath my fingers, I feel myself unraveling completely—lost in the vivid illusions of tasting her sweetness—the very essence of Kaitlyn Hawkins enveloping me.

As reality snaps back painfully with a shudder and gasp filling the silence of the room, I slump against the door. Heart still racing and breath short, I realize no amount of cold marble or whispered curses can erase what's ignited inside me. Kaitlyn Hawkins has marked me deeper than anyone ever has.

She's got me jacking off in the bathroom at a pool party for Christ's sake.

With shaky hands and a mind still reeling from intense release and vibrant images of Kaitlyn swimming in blue waters—of tasting more than just fantasies—I clean up and exit the bathroom.

Fuck me.

CHAPTER
TWO

Jake

AFTER THAT FATEFUL POOL PARTY, all bets are off. I'm like a madman.

I *stalk* Kaitlyn Hawkins. I follow her social media pages. I make a point to discreetly go places where I might see her. Hell, if I didn't know Nate had so many security cameras around his place, I'd break into her room and look for a diary or something.

Better yet, I'd put a camera up in there. So I could just watch her sleep.

But I'm not *that* crazy.

Not yet.

Instead, I hover at the edges of her world, a shadow she hasn't noticed—or maybe she just pretends not to.

Last night was another of those glittering events at the Hawkins Mansion. Nate threw one hell of a party, celebrating yet another win for the team. The lawn was scattered with high-profile guests, local celebrities, and a few of our teammates who could outdrink an entire bar. And then there was Kaitlyn, floating through the crowds like some ethereal goddess, laughing that musical laugh of hers that hooked deep into my guts.

She was wearing this little number, a shimmering gold dress that clung to every curve as if it revered her body. It made my mouth dry and every other part of me ache with want. I kept to the shadows, nursing a whiskey, watching her spin and twirl under the fairy lights strung up around the garden.

I'd give anything to be the reason for her smile. To be the one she looks at with those sparking hazel eyes full of mischief and lust. But every time I get close, Nate's there—big brother act in full force—reminding everyone who's within earshot that Kaitlyn is off limits.

And I supposed I should be grateful for that. Nate is keeping everyone else away from her.

The only problem is he's keeping *me* away from her too.

I'm parked across the street of their house tonight, drumming my fingers on my steering wheel, imagining what it would be like to just waltz through the doors and take her into my arms.

To kiss her…

I imagine she'd taste like *cherries*. Ripe and sweet. Her skin would be soft as I graze my lips down her neck. A soft intake of breath, maybe a little whimper.

Fuuuuck…

My cock is so hard it's about to burst through the seam of my pants, so I unzip myself and take it in my hand.

Thinking about her, just her, I start stroking slowly at first. And then faster. The urgency builds up inside me like a wildfire ready to consume everything in its path.

I picture her laughing at something I say, her head thrown back in delight, those lips parting as if inviting me to shut them up with a kiss that could promise the world and deliver hell at the same time. Her body pressed against mine as I explore every inch of her, each curve under my fingers burning my skin with desire.

And then in my mind's eye, she's pulling me towards her bedroom—the one place in the entire world I want to be right now. In my fantasy, there are no barriers, no Nate to cock-block me. Just Kaitlyn and me, tangled in sheets that whisper secrets with every friction.

Her hands are everywhere, pulling me closer, urging me to lose control. And boy, do I. I forget the rules, the world outside, everything but the feel of her beneath me. My hand moves faster over my length as I imagine driving into her wetness, hearing her moan my name like it's a prayer or maybe a curse.

I'm close now, so fucking close I can almost taste it—taste *her*.

I tilt my head back against the headrest of my car and close my eyes for a moment. The sound of my heavy breathing mixes with the fantasy echoes of Kaitlyn's moans.

With a final stroke, my release crashes over me like a tidal wave. I come hard and fast, groaning her name into the night air, filled with nothing but my ragged breaths and the faintest scent of jasmine from the gardens across the street.

I open my eyes slowly. The reality of the dark car interior greets me along with a sharp pang of guilt and frustration knotted together tight in my gut. It's maddening how much hold she has over me without even knowing it.

I wipe myself clean with some tissues from the glove compartment and tuck myself away. Glancing once more at the silhouette of the Hawkins Mansion under the moonlight makes my heart twitch uncomfortably.

"Fuck," I mutter under my breath as I start the car engine. A part of me is disgusted by this obsessive desire, but another part—a darker, much more honest part—whispers that it's far too late for regrets or what ifs.

Tonight was just another night of countless ones spent yearning from afar.

But something deep within tells me it won't be long before fantasies aren't enough—before I'm driven to do something about this inferno Kaitlyn unknowingly stoked in me.

CHAPTER
THREE

Kaitlyn

I SAUNTER through the buzzing crowd at Hawkins Stadium, the late afternoon sun casting a lazy glow over the field. The air is thick with the scent of popcorn and anticipation, but I'm not here for the game.

I'm here because it's where life seems to happen in our little town. And maybe, just maybe, because *he's* here.

"Go, Bulldogs!" someone shouts from behind me, and I can't help but roll my eyes. It's always about the Bulldogs, isn't it? Nate's team.

But as much as I want to deny it, my heart skips a beat every time they play. Not for the sport—hell no—but for the chance of spotting *him* again.

Jake. With his umpire uniform hugging his body in all the right places, he's like an accidental fantasy sprung to life in the middle of small-town America.

"Kaitlyn, over here!" I hear my name and turn to see a cluster of familiar faces waving me down. I flash them a grin and make my way over.

"Wouldn't miss it," I quip, sliding onto the bleacher with practiced ease. My gaze, though, instantly flickers back to the diamond, searching for that familiar stance—the way he holds himself when he's calling a shot.

"Your brother's on fire today," one of the girls comments, her eyes bright with excitement.

"Is he?" I feign interest, my lips curving into a smile that doesn't quite reach my eyes. Nate's athletic prowess is old news, but Jake...seeing him out there, authoritative and focused, sends a thrill straight through me. It's a dangerous game, this crush on my brother's friend.

Forbidden fruit never tasted so sweet, and I've been starving for a bite.

"Come on, Kaitlyn, pay attention!" another friend teases, nudging me playfully.

But I can't, not really. Not when every cell in my body is attuned to *him*, to the way his arms move as he signals another strike.

It's ridiculous, this pull he has on me. Even though I'm still a virgin, I've had boyfriends and crushes before. I mean, guys have come and gone, but none have stuck like this relentless attraction to Jake.

Every stolen glance, every brief conversation with him is etched into my memory, stoking the flames of a desire I'm not sure I can control.

"Damn," I murmur under my breath as he bends over to dust off home plate, giving the crowd a prime view of his assets. A flush creeps up my neck, and I fan myself with my hand, pretending it's the summer heat that's got me all hot and bothered.

"Hot out, isn't it?" I say to no one in particular, hoping my friends attribute my flushed cheeks to the weather rather than my raging hormones.

"Sure is," they agree, blissfully unaware of

the internal turmoil I'm experiencing. They chat away about post-game plans, but I barely register their words. My mind is busy painting scenarios that would make even the sultriest romance novels blush. Scenes of tangled sheets, whispered promises, and Jake looking at me like I'm the only girl in the world.

I internally chide myself, trying to shake away the images. But it's no use. He's under my skin, and I can't ignore it any longer. Maybe this time, I'll find a way to breach that invisible line between us.

Because if there's one thing Kaitlyn Hawkins isn't afraid of, it's going after what she wants.

And oh, do I want him.

As the final inning draws to a close and the roar of the crowd crescendos into a triumphant cheer, I find myself already edging toward the dugout. My heart races, adrenaline mixing with raw attraction. Nate's team has won, and the atmosphere is electric, charged with excitement and the sharp tang of victory. I clap my hands, my gaze locked on Jake as he makes his way off the field, his uniform clinging to his muscular frame in ways that command attention.

"Great game, Jake!" I call out, a little louder

than necessary, my voice lilting playfully. He glances up, those piercing blue eyes locking onto mine for a brief moment, sending a thrill spiraling down my spine. My breath catches as his lips quirk into a small smile before he returns to discussing some plays with another umpire.

Not wanting to miss my chance, I stride confidently towards him after he's done debriefing. The ground under my feet feels like clouds. I'm barely aware of anything but him. "Hey," I start, trying to sound casual but probably failing miserably. "You were really something out there today."

Jake wipes his brow with the back of his hand, and damn if even that small gesture doesn't seem sexy right now. "Thanks, Kaitlyn," he says in that deep voice that rumbles like distant thunder and seems to vibrate right through me. "Hot day for a game, huh?"

I nod vigorously, moving a step closer. "Definitely hot." I pause for emphasis, biting my lip slightly as I add, "But I think it just got hotter." Cheesy? Probably. But it earns me another of those half-smiles that tell me he's not entirely immune to my charms.

His chuckle is low and intimate. "Is that so?"

Encouraged by his tone, I lean in slightly. "Yeah. And you know what would cool everyone down? A celebration at my brother's place. He's throwing a victory party." It's bold to invite him without confirming with Nate first, but sometimes you have to take risks.

Jake raises an eyebrow—a look that's somehow both skeptical and intrigued. "Is Nate okay with his sister inviting rogue umpires over?"

"I'm sure he won't mind," I reply quickly, giving Jake a mischievous wink.

Seemingly convinced or perhaps just unwilling to resist the promise of more interactions laced with this palpable tension between us, Jake nods slowly. "Alright," he agrees mildly. "Sounds like a plan."

Flushed with success and the prospect of what the evening could bring—laughing under the stars and playing flirtatious games by the poolside—I pull out my phone and text Nate.

> Throwing post-game bash at
> your place. Invite your team!

By the time I look up from sending the

message, Jake's watching me with an intensity that suggests tonight might just be more eventful than any victory party could be on its own.

I sure hope so.

CHAPTER
FOUR

Jake

I'M LEANING against the cool marble countertop at Nate's after-game bash, trying to look casual. But let's be real—I'm on high alert, waiting for that telltale splash that signals Kaitlyn's diving into the pool. Weeks have dragged by, and it's like I've got this compass inside me that always points to her.

"Hey, Jake, you're zoning out, man!" Nate slaps my back, beer sloshing from his red cup. His eyes are lit up, that post-win adrenaline still pumping through him. I force a grin, clink my cup against his.

"Sorry, just thinking about some calls from the game," I lie smoothly.

But then there it is—the splash—and I forget how to breathe. Kaitlyn's laughter bubbles up, and I make some weak excuse about getting another drink so I can drift closer to where she's swimming. Her skin glistens in the moonlight, and God, those curves of hers could drive a man wild. I'm pulsing with need, and it's taking all I have not to jump in that water with her.

"Jake, you're not much of a swimmer, huh?" She pulls herself up onto the edge of the pool, water cascading off her like she's some kind of goddess.

"Never had the same allure for me as base-ball," I say, voice tight. It's true, but right now, watching her, I'm second-guessing all my life choices.

"Maybe you just haven't had the right coach." Her laugh is part challenge, part invita-tion. And damn if I don't want to accept it.

"Could be," I chuckle, playing it off while my body screams yes.

We're talking more these days—small chats that turned into long conversations. She's got this passion for photography, sees the world through lenses and light in ways I never considered. And when she talks about her latest adventure or the picture she's chasing, it lights something up in me too.

"Got this amazing shot yesterday," she says, pulling out her phone. "Sunrise over the river, you know?"

"Let's see it." I lean in close, and her scent wraps around me, fresh and sweet. The photo is stunning, the colors bleeding into each other like the sky's on fire. "That's...wow."

"Right? It was worth waking up at the crack of dawn." Her eyes meet mine, and there's this spark, like we're sharing a secret no one else gets.

"Definitely," I agree, our fingers brushing as she hands me the phone. That touch sends heat straight through me, and I'm harder than a foul ball.

"Jake, you okay?" She's looking at me with concern now, and I realize I'm gritting my teeth.

"Fine. Just, uh, need the bathroom." I excuse myself, heading inside, cursing under my breath for being such a mess around her.

I lock myself in the bathroom, images of Kaitlyn's wet body clouding my mind. My hand wraps around myself, and it's her name

I'm whispering as I chase release, quick and dirty. God, what she does to me.

I come, white spurts shooting out of me as I curse under my breath. Fuck, it seems all I do is clean cum splatters off my best friend's bathroom floor these days.

When I come back out, feeling equal parts relieved and ashamed, she's right there, chatting with someone else. But her eyes find mine across the crowd, and there's a curious tilt to her smile that makes me wonder what she knows.

"Enjoy your swim?" I tease, sidling up to her once she's alone again.

"Always do," she grins. "You should try it sometime."

"Maybe I will," I answer, and the promise hangs between us, heavy and charged.

Tonight, I'll leave with fantasies swirling in my head. But tomorrow, who knows? Maybe I'll take her up on that offer. After all, I'm already drowning in thoughts of her. Might as well get wet.

———

I'm leaning against the bar at Nate's place after another game, nursing a drink I don't really want. The summer night wraps around us like a sultry promise, but my mind is a goddamn war zone. Kaitlyn's laughter rings out from the pool, that carefree sound that's come to mean trouble for me. I shouldn't be here, shouldn't let her pull me in with that magnetic charm of hers.

"Hey, ump," she calls out, waving me over with a wet hand, droplets flying. "Come tell me if my dive was a perfect ten!"

She's joking, playing on my profession, but it's no joke how much I want to be the one to score every inch of her. My feet move before my brain gives permission and there I am, standing at the edge of the pool, trying not to stare as she surfaces, water streaming off her like some damn mermaid.

"Looked more like a solid eight to me," I banter back, grateful for the darkness hiding my clenched jaw and too-tight shorts.

"Harsh critic!" She pouts playfully, pushing wet strands of hair from her face, and hell if that doesn't make me imagine other scenarios where her hair would be just as wild, just as wet.

"Got to keep the standards high," I reply, but my voice betrays me and comes out rougher than intended.

Kaitlyn doesn't seem to notice. Or maybe she does, because suddenly she's pulling herself out of the pool, all graceful limbs and glistening skin, and I'm hit with an urge so strong it nearly buckles my knees. I should walk away, but instead, I'm frozen, watching her approach me in slow motion.

"Jake," she says softly, so close now I can feel the heat radiating from her body. "Why do you always watch me and never join in?"

Her question pierces through the haze of my desire, and I realize this is it—my moment of truth. Do I keep hiding behind the veil of friendship, or do I risk everything on this slip of a girl who's under my skin like a tattoo?

"Maybe I'm scared of getting burned," I admit, the words tumbling out raw and honest.

"A pool is cool—not hot," she points out. Her hazel eyes lock onto mine, filled with a daring that says she knows exactly what she's doing to me.

"It's refreshing" she whispers as she steps closer, close enough for me to catch the scent of chlorine mixed with her floral perfume.

"Maybe I'm afraid I'll be addicted once I try it," I confess, because it's true. I've played with fire before, got scorched enough times to know better. But Kaitlyn, she's a whole different kind of flame, and I'm not sure any amount of caution will save me from getting singed.

"Then let's be addicted together," she murmurs, and before I can process the implication, her lips are on mine.

It's a soft collision, a barely-there touch that has me reeling more than any deep plunge ever could. I'm kissing Kaitlyn Hawkins, and it feels like both a victory and a defeat. Her mouth moves against mine with a sweet urgency that screams innocence, but there's a flicker of something else there too—curiosity, maybe. Hunger, definitely.

I glance around, and the party is hopping so much, nobody seemed to have noticed our little indiscretion. Thank fuck.

The kiss ends too soon, leaving me gasping, addicted, and utterly screwed. I pull back, look into those wide eyes that seem to see right through me, and I know I'm done for.

"Fuck it," I say, voice heavy with a mix of lust and something dangerously close to tenderness. "Let's jump in with both feet."

I pick her up and jump into the pool.

Jake

I'M chest-deep in the pool's warm embrace, the golden hues of Nate's estate lighting up the night like it's trying to outshine the stars. Kaitlyn, with her sun-kissed skin and those hazel eyes that flicker with mischief, is a few strokes away.

"Care for a race?" I challenge, my voice carrying over the water.

She grins, playful as ever. "Only if you can handle losing."

The water surges around us as we kick off. But this isn't about winning. It's about the chase, about the electric thrill that zaps through me every time she looks back over her shoulder with that wild laughter bubbling from her lips.

We reach the other end together, panting, laughing, and it's like there's no one else here but us. Her giggles echo against the opulent backdrop, a sound so genuine it sends a shiver down my spine that's got nothing to do with the night air.

"Jake," she whispers, her fingers finding mine under the water. "Catch me if you can."

It's all the invitation I need. My body reacts before my mind catches up, desire pooling in my veins as heavy as lead. We're underwater ballet dancers, all fluid movements and silent communication. It's a discreet dance of hips meeting hips, a push and pull that makes my heart slam against my ribs.

My cock is hard, and she backs that pretty little ass against me and rubs it. I hump her as discreetly as I can under the water. Something about doing this here with all these people around makes the moment even that much more exciting.

"Kaitlyn," I rasp, barely above a breath, and I can feel the heat rising between us, the kind of heat that has nothing to do with the summer night.

"Shh," she places a finger on my lips, her smile wicked. "Not here."

She glides out of the pool, water cascading off her like she's some kind of goddess stepping out of her element. I follow, utterly spellbound. She leads me by the hand across the lush grass, our footfalls silent. The mansion looms before us, grand and imposing, but with Kaitlyn tugging me forward, there's no way I can say no.

Hell no.

The door to her room clicks shut behind us, sealing us away from the rest of the world. Her gaze locks onto mine, fierce and unyielding. "Welcome to my sanctuary," she says, her voice threaded with promises.

And I'm ready to worship at her altar.

I'm on fire, and Kaitlyn's touch is both the spark and the kindling. Her room is a haven of soft light and softer sheets, and we're all over each out, shedding clothes like they're on fire.

"Jake," she whispers against my neck, her breath hot and heavy. "Show ,e."

"Only if you show me first," I challenge

back, grinning despite the throb of desire that courses through me.

She meets my eyes, that mischievous glint in hers saying she's ready to play. With a sly smile, she pushes me down onto the bed. The hunger in her gaze matches the pounding rhythm in my chest as she trails kisses down my body, exploring with an eager curiosity that has my fingers digging into the sheets.

"Kaitlyn," I gasp as she takes me into her mouth, warm and wet and oh so perfect. God, she's a natural, sending shivers of pleasure down my spine.

I'm not one to be outdone. Flipping us over, I pin her beneath me, my hands roaming her sun-kissed skin. She tastes like chlorine and temptation, and when I return the favor, her moans fill the room. It's a melody I could listen to forever, but tonight's about more than just this.

"Are you sure?" I ask, voice husky as I hover above her now. I need to hear it. I need to know she wants this as much as I do.

"More than anything," she breathes out, and that's all the confirmation I need.

Slow and steady, I guide myself into her,

watching Kaitlyn's face for any sign of discomfort. There's a flicker, a brief wince, but then she's pulling me closer, wrapping her legs around me, urging me deeper. And damn, the feeling of her tight around me—it's like nothing else.

"Jake..." she whispers, and that's all it takes.

We move together, lost in the heat and the rush. Her pussy is grippin me so damn tight. "Fuck baby, how are you so tight?" I manage to croak out.

Her cheeks turn pink as she confesses, "Because this is my first time."

I go completely still as I stare down at her, trying to process the magnitude of the gift she's given me.

"Motherfucker," I grunt out as I finally snap and drive my hips back and forth, fucking into her ferociously as my mind churns with thoughts of possession.

Mine, mine, mine!

Kaitlyn is *mine*.

"I'm not going to last long, baby. I need you to come for me. Can you do that, you pretty little thing?"

I reach down and flick my thumb over her clit, and Kaitlyn goes off beautifully.

Her pussy flutters around me as she screams and clutches onto me, and then I lose it.

And when I come, it's like hitting a home run in Hawkins Stadium—exhilarating, triumphant, and damn satisfying. I ride her through our orgasms, pumping every last bit of cum from my balls into her until it's dripping down onto the bed.

But then I hear a sound like strikes the fear of God into me.

It's Nate, and he's mad as hell.

"What the fuck do you think you're doing?"

CHAPTER
SIX

Kaitlyn

THE DOOR SLAMS OPEN. Heat floods my cheeks, and I'm scrambling for the sheet, trying to shield my nakedness from Nate's blazing green eyes. Jake's heavy breath hitches against my neck, and I can feel his heart hammering, a wild rhythm that matches my own.

"Jesus, Kaitlyn!" Nate's voice is a whip crack in the opulent bedroom of the Hawkins estate. The scent of roses does nothing to mask the thick aroma of sex hanging in the air.

"Fuck, Nate, I..." My words trip over themselves, lost in the chaos.

He doesn't hear me. His gaze, sharp as the pitches he's famous for, skewers Jake. "Are you planning on marrying my sister, or are you just fucking around?"

Jake stiffens above me, and it's not just his body that freezes. It's his soul, his everything. I search his piercing blue eyes for something, anything, that speaks of our tangled sheets and whispered promises.

But he's silent. A statue. And those eyes that I've drowned in a thousand times over are suddenly shallow pools I can't read.

I shove at Jake's chest, a desperate need to escape clawing its way up my throat. I stumble out of bed, grabbing whatever clothing I can find. My heart pounds, a frantic drumbeat drowning out the shouting match brewing behind me.

I run, barefoot, down the grand staircase, each step echoing like a gavel sentencing me for sins of the flesh and heart. I'm outside now, the manicured lawns a blur under the moonlight, my tears mixing with the night's dew.

Guilt claws at me with sharp talons. Guilt

for what I've done to Nate, for the sacred bond I've tarnished.

And Jake... oh God, Jake. Was I just a conquest? A fling for the umpire who calls fair and foul with unerring precision but couldn't give me a straight answer when it mattered most?

"Shit," I whisper into the darkness, the word stark against the silence of the estate. Nate's estate. Where I've always been the little sister, the princess in the tower. And now, I'm just Kaitlyn, the girl who might have mistaken lust for love.

I collapse into a heap and sob, tears streaming down my face.

What have I done?

———

I slam the door of my car with a force that mirrors the chaos in my chest. My hands shake as I grip the steering wheel, knuckles white, breaths coming in short, sharp gasps that match the erratic thumping of my heart.

I shut my eyes tight and try to summon the cold detachment I desperately need. It's been three days, and I still can't shake him.

Memories flash like lightning—Jake's touch, his skin against mine, the way he made me feel alive and wanted. But that's all they are now, memories tainted by the sting of betrayal and doubt.

I don't know how long I drive. I don't even know where I'm going. And this is what I've done ever since that night I gave Jake my virginity.

I drive, and then I wind back up at home at Nate's mansion. I still haven't talked to my brother. I can't. The shame eats at me.

Not shame for what I've done. I don't regret being with Jake. No, I'm ashamed that he doesn't want me forever. That I was just a one night stand to him.

So, I avoid my brother. I don't come home until I know he's gone.

My room feels foreign as I step inside, a sanctuary breached by the ghost of Jake's presence. I toss my keys on the dresser and head straight for the shower, eager for anything to wash away my feelings.

Hot water pelts my skin, but it can't wash away the doubt seared into my mind. The image of Jake freezing, his piercing blue eyes wide with something akin to fear, burns behind my eyelids.

I watch the steam as it twists and turns before disappearing. I don't want him to feel like I'm *that* girl, the one trying to trap him into something.

The way he froze…it was humiliating.

I wrap myself in a towel, the fabric a barrier between myself and the world.

I slip into bed, the cool sheets a contrast to the lingering warmth on my skin. Closing my eyes, I summon a mask of indifference, an armor forged from the hurt and humiliation of that night.

Sleep doesn't come easy, but when it does, it's devoid of dreams. No whispers of desire, no illusion of love. Just darkness—a welcome reprieve from the mess of my reality.

When morning comes, I rise with a single purpose. Retreat from love. Shields up.

I'm done with Jake Reynolds.

He's just another strikeout in a game I'm no longer playing.

CHAPTER
SEVEN

Jake

THE CROWD BUZZES WITH ANTICIPATION, but my heart's pounding out a different rhythm. I'm not seeing the diamond, the fans, or the players—there's only Kaitlyn up in the stands, her blonde hair catching the stadium lights like a halo.

"Play ball!" someone shouts, but I don't budge. Screw protocol.

"Sorry folks," I say into the mic, my voice echoing around Hawkins Stadium. "There's something I gotta do."

I toss the mic down and hustle across the

field, eyes fixed on Kaitlyn. I can't believe she's finally here. She hasn't been at the last three games, and it's been killing me. I tired to readh her phone, but I kept getting sent straight to voicemail.

I couldn't go over to Nate's. Not only is he still pissed at me, but I didn't know if Kaitlyn would even see me. The way she ran out of the room that night like she was ashamed of what we'd done…

It tore me up inside. I've been a wreck ever since.

All I can think about is her.

And now that she's here, I'm not letting her slip away again.

I glance over at Nate, and he's glaring at me, but I don't give a fuck. He might be my best friend, but his little sister is my eveything, and I can no longer live without her.

Her gaze meets mine, trepidation written all over that beautiful face.

"Kaitlyn Hawkins!" I call out to her.

Her eyes are wide. She looks terrified, but I can't stop now. No matter what her answer is.

"I am so in love with you, and I need you more than I've ever needed anything! You are my world, beautiful. I need you to know that!"

I'm at the edge of the field now, right below her seat. Without another second's hesitation, I drop to one knee. The crowd gasps, a wave of whispers crescendoing into a roar.

"Kaitlyn Hawkins," I say, loud enough so every last person hears me over their excitement. "Will you marry me?"

Her hands fly to her mouth, those hazel eyes wide with shock.

There's a long moment when she doesn't say anything.

"You want me?" she asks me, and I frown at the surprise in her voice.

"Hell fucking yes, baby. Why would you ever doubt that."

Her bottom lip trembles. "You froze," she whispers, and then it dawns on me.

I want to kick myself in the ass. When Nate asked me if I was going to marry her, I was so shocked and overjoyed at the prospect, I couldn't speak.

"Baby, I was going to tell him yes, but then you ran out of the room, and I thought you regretted us."

Kaitlyn starts crying, and then a smile blooms on her face as she shakes her head and finally says, "Yes!"

I'm damn near sobbing in relief too when she leaps over the railing like she's done it a hundred times, sprinting onto the field, and into my arms.

She crashes into me, and I catch her, spinning her around. When I finally stop, our lips crash together, hungry and unapologetic. The stadium erupts, but all I hear is the rush of blood in my ears. All I feel are Kaitlyn's eager kisses.

"Let's get out of here," I murmur against her lips.

"Lead the way," she breathes, all mischief and fire.

We tear away from the field, leaving cheers and whistles behind us. Once inside the locker room, I pin her against the cold metal lockers. Our breaths mix, ragged and hot as clothes tear away, revealing skin that's flushed and aching for each other's touch.

"Jake, I need you," she moans, and I answer with actions, not words.

Her back presses against the lockers, her hands tugging at my hair as I trail kisses down her neck. Her pulse thrums under my lips, fast and erratic, matching the rhythm of our breathing.

"Right here, right now," Kaitlyn whispers, her voice a husky melody that drives me wild. I lift her up effortlessly, her legs wrapping around my waist as she clings to me. The cool metal of the locker sends shivers down her spine as I fuck deeper, driven by an insatiable need.

"Mine," I grunt out. "This little pussy is mine. Only mine."

Kaitlyn whimpers in response.

I grab a fistful of her hair and tug. "Don't you ever run from me again," I warn her. "This is where you belong. Right here on my cock. You hear me?"

The room seems to spin around us, the only reality being the heat of Kaitlyn's skin and the desperate sounds filling the air. I'm lost in her, in the feel, taste, and scent of her. Everything else—the game, the crowd, even time itself—melts away until there's nothing left but us.

"God, Jake," she gasps as I move with a fervor fueled by days of pent-up desire and longing. Each movement is more intense than the last, pushing us both towards an edge that seems both terrifying and inevitable.

Our eyes lock, and there's a silent agreement in their depths—a promise not just of tonight but of something deeper, something permanent. She bites her lip, and that's what does it for me.

"Oh, fuck, baby, here I come," I tell her as I feel my nut climbing up my stalk before it releases in a torrent into her soaking wet pussy that starts fluttering around me.

As we come together, Kaitlyn's cries echo off the walls, mingling with my own hoarse shout. The world snaps back into brutal clarity as we cling to each other, gasping for air in the aftermath of our storm.

Panting heavily, I rest my forehead against hers. "I meant what I said out there," I manage between breaths. "I can't lose you again."

Kaitlyn smiles softly, her fingers tracing idle patterns on my back. "You're not going to lose me," she reassures me. "You've got me for life now."

We dress slowly in the new quiet of the locker room. When we emerge into the night air outside Hawkins Stadium, it's like stepping into a new chapter of our lives—one filled with endless possibilities and promises made under stadium lights.

EPILOGUE

Three years later

Jake

"OKAY, munchkin, time to dazzle Uncle Nate with that gummy smile," I say as I juggle our baby girl in one arm as Kaitlyn locks up the car. Her laughter is a melody that dances on the breeze, and for a moment, I'm floored by how much I love these two—my girls.

"Jake, you do realize she's already got him wrapped around her tiny finger, right?" Kaitlyn teases, adjusting the diaper bag on her shoulder as we approach Nate's front door.

"Of course, but practice makes perfect." I wink at her, my heart swelling in my chest. Our little lady has the best of us both—Kaitlyn's sun-streaked locks and my stubborn chin.

Nate swings open the door before we even knock, his grin wide and welcoming. "There's my favorite niece!" he booms, scooping her from my arms and into his. The sight of this big, burly pitcher turned gentle giant always cracks me up.

It didn't take long before Nate came around to the idea of Kaitlyn being with me. Of course, the media's approval didn't hurt anything. I think Nate was just worried about his sister and being a protective big brother.

Which I can't blame him.

"Hey, don't get too comfortable there, champ. We're coming back for her later," I remind him, playfully punching his shoulder.

"Wouldn't dream of keeping her," Nate chuckles, but his eyes are already softening like he's considering it. "You kids go have fun. Leave the parenting to the pro."

"Pro, huh?" Kaitlyn raises an eyebrow, the twinkle in her eye telling me she's ready for our night out. It's been ages since we've done this—just us, no diapers, no feedings, just her hand in mine and the promise of a few stolen hours.

"Yup! Now shoo. Lovebirds need their time," Nate says with a mock sternness that doesn't quite reach his gaze. He's turning toward the opulent living room, all high ceilings and laughter echoing off the walls, his protective presence a fortress against any possible harm.

"Be good, angel," I call out, and our daughter rewards me with a bubbly giggle that echoes after us as we walk away.

"Think she'll be okay without us?" Kaitlyn asks, her voice threaded with the strain of every new parent.

"Baby, she's with Nate. She'll be ruling the mansion by the time we pick her up," I reassure her, my fingers lacing with hers as we head down the cobblestone path.

"True," she sighs, leaning into me. "So, Mr. Umpire, where are you taking me tonight? Somewhere I can let loose?"

"Thought we'd start with dinner at that new Italian place, then maybe hit the boardwalk. Win you a teddy bear or something cheesy like that," I say, my lips curving into a smirk.

"Ooh, Jake Reynolds, you do know the way to a girl's heart," she laughs, her hazel eyes shining with mischief and something warmer, deeper—a flame that's only grown over the years.

"Only yours, Kaitlyn," I whisper, my breath catching as she stands on tiptoe to press her lips to mine, soft and sweet and promising more.

"Let's make it a night to remember, then," she murmurs against my mouth, and I'm struck by the fierce certainty that, with her, every moment is unforgettable.

"Count on it, babe," I reply.

Tonight, it's just Kaitlyn and me—and nothing else matters.

———

The click of the front door shutting behind us echoes like a starter pistol. The night's still young, but the real fun's about to begin. Kaitlyn's got that look in her eyes—the one that says she's all mine and ready for anything I've got.

"Jake," she breathes out my name like it's a fucking lifeline, her back pressed against the wall, her chest heaving.

"Shh," I hush her gently, my lips trailing

down her neck, tasting the salt of her skin. "Tonight's about you, babe."

I lift her in my arms as though she weighs nothing, carrying her up the stairs with less effort than it takes to call a strike. Our bedroom's dark, but I know every inch of it. It's our sanctuary, where we shed the roles of parents and professionals, where it's just man and woman, raw and real.

"God, Jake," she whimpers as I lay her down on the bed, her body spread out before me like the finest feast. "Please."

"Patience, Kaitlyn," I chuckle lowly, my fingers unbuttoning her dress with practiced ease. Her breath catches. Anticipation ramps up another notch. Every piece of clothing that drops to the floor is a promise of what's to come.

Naked now, she's fucking magnificent. My gaze worships every curve, every scar, every inch of her that's seen life and love and pain. But it's between those thighs that I find my religion.

I take my time, kissing and licking my way slowly down her boy.

My *wife*.

"Jake, don't tease," she pleads, her hips lifting off the mattress, seeking my touch.

"Never," I whisper against her thigh before my tongue finally gives her what we both want. I eat her out like it's my last meal on earth, savoring the taste of her, the slick heat that coats my tongue. She grips the sheets, her moans filling the room, sweet music to my ears.

"Fuck, yes..." Her words dissolve into cries as I work her over, my mouth relentless, worshipful. I'm lost in her, drowning in the feel, the taste, the sound of her coming undone beneath me.

And she's still better that I ever imagined. Swear to god, it gets better every time I touch her.

"Jake... Jake, I'm—" Her thighs tremor around my head, her climax hitting her like a home run.

And right there, in the quiet aftermath, I know this—this passion, this love—is the fulfillment I've been searching for all my life.

I pull back to look at her. Kaitlyn's flushed and disheveled—beautiful in her raw, undone state. Her chest rises and falls rapidly, and those hazel eyes of hers are clouded with lust and love. Love for *me*. It's a look that punches straight through my chest every damn time.

I climb up her body slowly, savoring the feel of her skin against mine, the heat from her pouring into me, making me feel alive in ways that nothing else ever could. She wraps her arms around my neck, pulling me down for a fierce kiss that tastes like promise and wild things.

"More," she whispers against my lips, a playful yet demanding twinkle in her eyes. "I want more, Jake."

With a grin that feels like it's splitting my face wide open, I align myself with her entrance, teasing just the tip inside. "You sure you can handle more?" I tease back, enjoying the slight frustration that flickers across her face before turning into outright need.

"Try me," she challenges, biting her lip in that way that drives me absolutely insane.

I push in then, slowly at first to enjoy the gasp that escapes her, then harder, deeper. She meets every one of my thrusts with one of her own, our rhythm as perfect as a well-played game. The sound of our bodies coming together mingles with our moans and breaths, creating a symphony of sounds that could only belong to us.

"God, Kaitlyn," I manage to get out between thrusts. "You feel so fucking incredible."

She responds by raking her nails down my back, sending shivers trailing down my spine. "Only for you," she says breathlessly. "Always for you."

The pace builds frantically from there as we chase our release together. I hook one of her legs over my arm to drive deeper and she screams out in pleasure. The room is thick with the scent of sex and sweat and love—a tangible reminder of what we create together whenever we come together like this.

As we reach the edge, I press my forehead to hers, looking into those mesmerizing eyes as we climax together. Her inner walls clench around me as she arches off the bed, our names mingling on our lips like a sacred vow.

We collapse together in a tangle of limbs on the soaked sheets, both panting hard but grinning like fools. I roll over, pulling her into my arms so she can lay her head on my chest. Her hand finds its usual spot over my heart—the place she claims reminds her just how alive this love makes us both feel.

"Love you," I murmur into her hair as I kiss the top of her head.

"Love you more," she mutters back sleepily.

And as we drift off to sleep wrapped up in each other's arms in our little haven away from the world outside—it hits me hard all over again just how damn lucky I am to have this woman by my side.

Want a free book from Emma Bray? Go to www.authoremmabray.com.

Keep reading for an excerpt from The Baseball Player's Obsession:

Nate

I huff out a breath as I meander along the sidewalk. My latest conversation with my sister is still fresh in my mind.

Is this how I made her feel all those times

that I busted her balls over closing herself off and not giving any guy a chance?

I used to harp at Ella, but always with good intentions. I saw how lonely my sister secretly was, and I'm so glad that she finally gave Jesse Hamilton, the renowned basketball star, a chance.

They're married now, and all is well in paradise with a baby on the way. My sister has even talked her husband into letting her have a cat. He's not crazy about the furry felines himself, but she has him wrapped around her pretty little finger. The six-foot-six giant turns to mush in her hands.

I can't stop the grin that twitches my lips. That's exactly what I wanted for her.

And I'm happy for her, but now that Cindy has found her own happiness, she's determined to make sure I do likewise. Almost every time we talk, she tries to have a heart-to-heart with me and tell me I'm just like she was—that I shut myself off from everyone.

That's not true, though. I go on plenty of dates, and Cindy never even dated. There's a difference.

But she is right when she points out that I never allow myself to get close to any one woman. About two weeks is a woman's shelf life in my calendar. Once the fun is over, I put her back where she came from before things can get emotional and sticky. It's not that I'm one of those asshole guys who just wants to play the field or sow his wild oats.

I know what it is. Deep down, I'm afraid of ending up like our father.

All Cindy sees when she thinks about our father is how he abandoned us. But I see the deeper picture. I see a man who loved so hard that when he lost the love of his life, it broke him.

When our mom died of cancer when we were just little kids, our dad died right along with her. He couldn't cope, so he turned to booze to black out his feelings, and in the process, he abandoned his children.

Yeah, I was bitter about it like Cindy for a while, but I can't even hate him for it anymore. Instead, I just feel a deep well of pity, and it scares me. I don't ever want to love so hard that it destroys me to lose the person. It's better off to be alone than have that happen.

Whereas Cindy wouldn't date for fear that the person would abandon her, I don't like to get attached for fear that I'll end up just like my father. Loving so hard that it wrecks me.

I scowl to myself. I don't like dwelling on this shit. I wish Cindy would just drop it.

I feel a prickle of guilt when I realize this is probably exactly how she felt when I used to nag at her, but that's different. I'm the older brother. It was my job to encourage her to take her happiness.

Cindy's issues lay within she didn't think she was good enough for anyone to stick around. Mine are more like trying to protect myself and others. It's not the same, right?

A little bell jangles overhead as I walk into the pet store where Cindy and Jesse buy their cat food. Cindy is a total psychopath about that damn cat. She will only buy this special food from this certain pet shop, and Jesse has a game tonight, but their little furball needs food.

So, here I am buying little Fluffy her food. Go figure. Looks like my sister has me wrapped around her little redheaded finger too.

Oh, well. I guess this is what big brothers are for. It's not like I was doing anything else tonight. I've already had baseball practice, and our game isn't until the weekend, so I'm free for now.

The shop is fairly empty. There's only one old lady browsing the shelves when I walk in. I don't know where the worker is. Probably in the back doing some stuff. It doesn't look like the shop is overly busy with customers right now.

I walk over to the cat food aisle and look for the special food that Cindy claims is the only food that spoiled princess cat can eat.

Jesus, if she and Jesse are like this over a damn cat, I can only imagine what they're going to be like over their child.

My eyes scan the shelves. There are so many different kinds, and I can't remember exactly what the brand my sister says it was. Kitten something or was it Fancy something?

Hell, I don't know.

"Can I help you?" a sweet, feminine voice says from behind me.

I whirl around only to have my chest seize up like I'm having a heart attack.

I go completely still as my pulse stops and then skyrockets. I feel the blood rushing throughout my veins as I stare into a pair of midnight blue eyes. They're so blue they almost appear violet and otherworldly.

I'm looking down because this girl is impossibly short and tiny, yet she's a curvy little thing with just enough flair of hips and generous mounds for breasts to drive a man wild. Her hair is raven black and flows down her back in thick, luscious waves—all the way down to that impossibly tiny waist.

My god, she looks like some sort of little doll with her pale porcelain skin and those big midnight blue eyes framed by dark lashes. The paleness of her skin makes her little puffy pink lips appear that much brighter.

I'm staring at her, my throat tight, when her little brow furrows, and she licks her lips. My eyes home in on the motion of her pink tongue moistening her puffy flesh, and I feel myself hardening in my pants.

I bite back a groan and tear my gaze back up to her innocent-looking eyes. Fuck, this girl still looks like a teenager. I'm not old at twenty-six, but I'm probably too old to be having these thoughts about her.

I swallow, my throat working as I realize she's still waiting for an answer. "Do you work here?" I ask, sounding like the complete idiot I am. Of course, she fucking works here. She just asked me if I needed help.

Yes, I do need help, baby. I'm rendered completely immobile by you.

She smiles at me, her eyes twinkling. "You could say that. I'm the owner."

I blink, taken aback but strangely relieved. She must be at least eighteen in order to own this joint.

She must see the surprise in my eyes because she offers softly, "My parents left it to me when they died."

I know I shouldn't pry, but I can't help myself. I want to know everything about this girl. "How did they die?"

"A car accident a few years ago," she says before she shakes her head and looks past me toward the shelves. "Looking for some cat food?"

My heart aches for her because I recognize the look of an orphan in her eyes. It's the same look me and my sister had when my mom died and then our dad left us.

I cast my eyes back over the many brands on the shelf. "Yeah, it's for my sister's cat, but I can't remember what kind she said, and apparently this cat is picky as shit and will only eat this one type of food."

The raven-haired beauty throws her head

back and laughs before she asks, "What's your sister's name? If she's a regular here, I might know her and remember what she buys."

"Cindy," I tell her. Her eyes instantly light with recognition, and a smile breaks across her face as she reaches out and grabs a can of cat food and shows it to me. "This is what her kitten likes."

I take the can from her and then grab several more. "Thanks...?" I raise a questioning brow at her, prompting her for her name. My eyes have already studied her chest long enough to know she's not wearing a name badge.

"Brandy," she offers me her name with a smile that causes my chest to ache painfully again.

"Brandy," I repeat her name, loving the way it rolls off my tongue. "I'm Nate."

She blushes as she smiles again. "Nice to meet you Nate, Cindy's brother."

My cock is a steel rod now. Hearing my name in her innocently sultry voice is almost enough to make me nut all in my jeans right here.

I follow her to the counter, admiring her ass like any red-blooded male would do. The way those jeans hug that succulent peach of an ass so perfectly....

The way those long locks sway against her back...

My fingers twitch around the cans. I'm suddenly fighting the undeniable urge to fists my hands in that hair. I have visions of me plowing into her with my hands buried in her hair, my lips smashed over her beautiful bee-stung lips, and I feel my cock aching, my balls harder than stones.

Fuck, I have never been this hard up for a woman before—especially one I just met.

"So, you're a baseball player," Brandy comments as she rings up the cat food.

I raise an eyebrow. "Cindy has been talking about me?"

She laughs. "Only every time she comes in here."

I roll my eyes. "No telling what she's saying about me."

"It's all good. I promise." She gives me that heart-stoppingly beautiful smile again, and it's enough to make my breath catch. Fuck, this girl is so damn beautiful.

The things she's doing to my body and chest are really fucking with my head. I want to ask her out, and I'm never shy, but the words stick in my throat. What the fuck? I've never been the guy who hesitates, but something about Brandy has me all tied up in knots.

She puts the receipt in the bag and then hands it to me. My fingers brush hers as I take it from her.

Our eyes meet as electricity snaps between us. Her eyes widen slightly, her lips parting as she stares at me.

I swallow. Fuck, does she feel it too?

She bites her lip and looks up at me from beneath those thick lashes, and all I can do is stare at the way her teeth pierce the flesh, wishing that it was me nibbling on that lip.

I finally break our staring contest before I do something crazy like lean across this counter and taste those sweet lips that are calling to me.

The old lady shuffles up behind me and claims Brandy's attention with a warm welcome that lets me know she's a regular customer here too.

Brandy pulls her eyes away from me and smiles kindly at the old lady, effectively dismissing me.

I try to ignore the pang that causes me.

When her gaze leaves mine, I feel like I've lost something precious.

I walk out of the store, my feet feeling heavier with every step I take away from her.

I stop outside and turn to look back in and admire her beautiful form as she helps the old lady with her purchases.

Something stirs inside me the longer I watch Brandy. It's something I've never felt before.

Something dark and dangerous.

Something that scares the shit out of me.

And when I try to pull myself away from the window, my feet won't move.

My eyes are glued to her. I can't seem to look away, even though I'm trying with all my might.

I swallow hard as realization creeps over me.

I am so fucked.

9 798822 719547